The Looking Book

Written and Illustrated
by P.K. Hallinan

 CHILDRENS PRESS, CHICAGO

Library of Congress Cataloging in Publication Data

Hallinan, P   K
  The looking book.

  SUMMARY: Torn away from the television by their
mother, two children discover some delights in the
outdoors.
  [1. Nature—Fiction.   2. Stories in rhyme]
I. Title.
PZ8.3.H15Lo   [E]   73-6573
ISBN 0-516-03520-7

1 2 3 4 5 6 7 8 9 10 11 12 13 14 15 16 17 18 19 20 21 22 23 24 25 R 75 74 73

the Looking Book

"Turn off that darn T.V.!"
Mommy said one day,
"Go on outside...
go outside and play!"

"But we're watching cartoons!"
Kenny said with a pout,
"And there's nothing to do
if you make us go out!"

And Mikey said....

"There's nothing to do
        and nothing to see,
we want to stay here
        and watch the T.V."

But Mommy just smiled
through all their sad sighs,
and when they were done,
she held out a surprise.

A very strange surprise...

they looked just like glasses,
but bigger by far,
with air where the
   lenses
usually are.

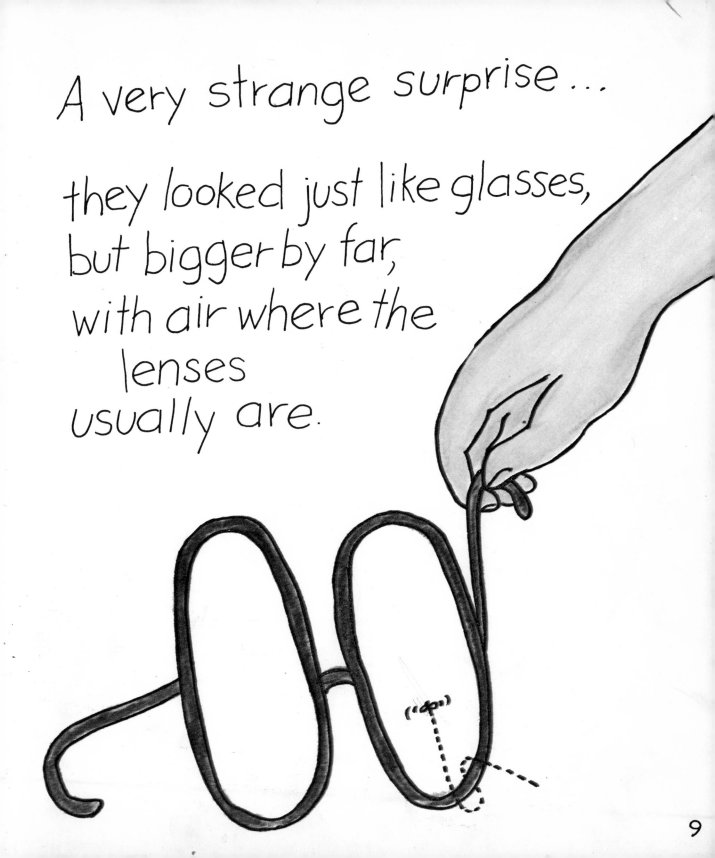

"What are they?" asked Kenny,
taking hold of his prize.
"Do I eat them, or bounce them,
or put them on my eyes?"

"They're lookers," said Mommy
just as plain as can be.
"They help you to look...
they help you to see."

So go on outside,
go out the back door,
and look with your lookers
like you've never looked
before."

On out the back door,
to the wide open spaces,
they marched with their
                    lookers
in place on their faces.

And it didn't take long to find something to see. Within only seconds, Mikey found a great tree.

"Look at this!" Mikey said, shouting with glee. "Look at this wonderful, beautiful tree!"

"It's wide and it's tall... and the leaves are all green.

This is the best tree that I've ever seen!"

16

Then they looked at each other
and smiled in kind,
and decided to see
what else they could find.

So, they both went out looking....

and Kenny sat down
on a small patch of ground
and parted the grass
that grew all around.

"This grass is amazing!"
he suddenly said.
"There are all kinds of
things here...
brown, yellow and red!"

There are twig-things and rock-things... and dirt-things and string-things... not to mention a whole lot of little black thing-things!"

And then Mikey said...

"There are lots of great
bugs, too...
going every which way!
They don't sing or dance,
but they're great anyway!"

Then he reached down
and picked up
an old wooden stick,
and yelled out to Kenny
"You better come quick!"

"There's a lady bug here
on this piece of wet wood...
it's not wearing a bow-tie or a
funny red hood...
but it's doing
all the
things a
lady bug
should!
And better than
any cartoon
bug could!"

But Kenny was too busy to come.

He stood by a rose bush
smelling a rose,
and held the small flower
right under his nose.

He sniffed it and
whiffed it,
and let out a sigh
and fell on the lawn
with a breathless "Oh, my!"

Then
he said...

"This rose doesn't smile,
or wear pretty clothes,
but it's really one heck
of a beautiful rose!"

Mikey was off
somewhere else again...

"Oh look!" he yelled out,
pointing up at the sky,
"An honest to goodness
real live butterfly!"

"For being half butter,
      the other half fly,
    it looks really nice
      up there in the sky!"

"I just don't believe it!"
kenny said suddenly...
"There's so much to look at,
so much to see!
I just never knew
there was so much to do!"

And so
they looked
high...

they looked low...

they looked very hard...

they looked with their lookers all over the yard.

And it wasn't till later,
when dinner was cooking,
that Kenny and Mikey
finally stopped looking.

With lookers in hand,
and eyes big and round,
they went into the house
and told what they'd found.

And they said...

"There were tree-things
and bee-things
and dandylions and
weeds...

there were small things
and tall things,
and flowers with seeds...
there were all Kinds
of new things,
green, purple and
blue things...

there was every kind
    of <u>do</u>-<u>thing</u>
any place ever needs!"

"It was the greatest day ever!"
They said with a shout...
"And first thing tomorrow,
we're going back out!"

They gave their lookers
back to Mommy...

and then
they said...

"And you want to know
        something...
the best part of all?
You don't need the lookers,
you don't need them at all!

'Cause that's the <u>very</u> best thing...
the best thing about them....
you don't have to wear them,
you can see things
without them!"

ABOUT THE AUTHOR/ARTIST: Patrick Hallinan first began writing for children at the request of his wife, who asked him to write a book as a Christmas present for their two young sons. With the publication of his second book, Mr. Hallinan, through his charming text and pictures, shares with all children his delight in the world around him. He lives in southern California.